SNIP SNAP CROC

Library of Congress Control Number: 2006038442

ISBN 978 1 84538 998 7

Written by Caroline Castle
Edited by Clare Weaver
Designed by Alix Wood
Illustrated by Andrew Crowson

Printed in China

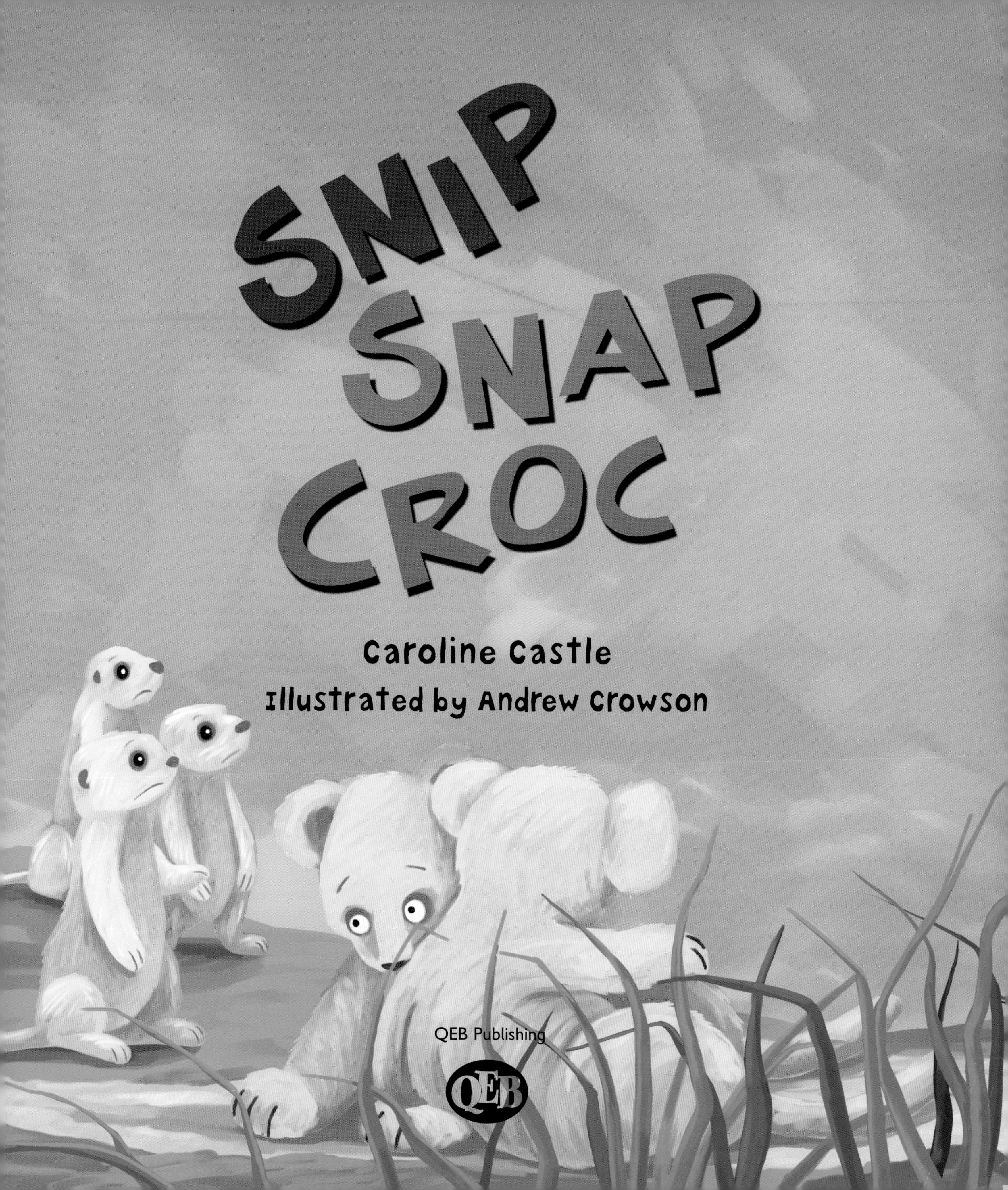

SNIP SNAP CROC

Caroline Castle

Illustrated by Andrew Crowson

QEB Publishing

QEB

In a faraway land in Africa,

where the
sun shines
all day long,

there is a big river called the Nile.

One morning,
lying lazily on its
sandy banks was...

Snip Snap Croc!

She swished her huge tail and sang
out to all the creatures on the shore.
Her crocodile voice made them shiver.

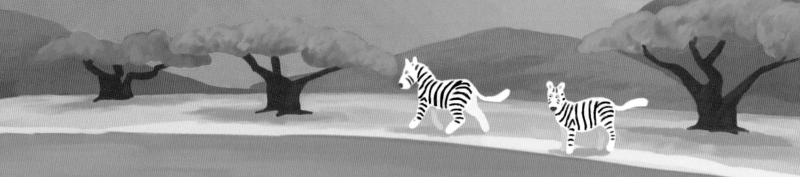

"My name is Snip Snap Croc,
I am so fine!
With these big, sharp teeth of mine!
All of them go

snip snap snip!

Come too close and I'll

nip nip nip!"

In the tall tree, Mama Baboon shivered and told her baby, "Don't go near Snip Snap Croc, all right? She'll eat you up with one big bite.

So, listen to Mama and stay close by, for I love you more than the mountain high."

In the bushes, Mama Meerkat told her little ones,

"Oh, stay away from that crocodile
who calls to us from the banks of the Nile.
Don't wander off, keep in my sight,
for I love you more than the stars so bright."

And in the long grass, Mama Lion told her bouncy little cubs,

"It's lunchtime soon and nasty Snip Snap would eat you up for a tasty snack.
So, don't stray far from Mama's side,
for I love you more than the ocean wide."

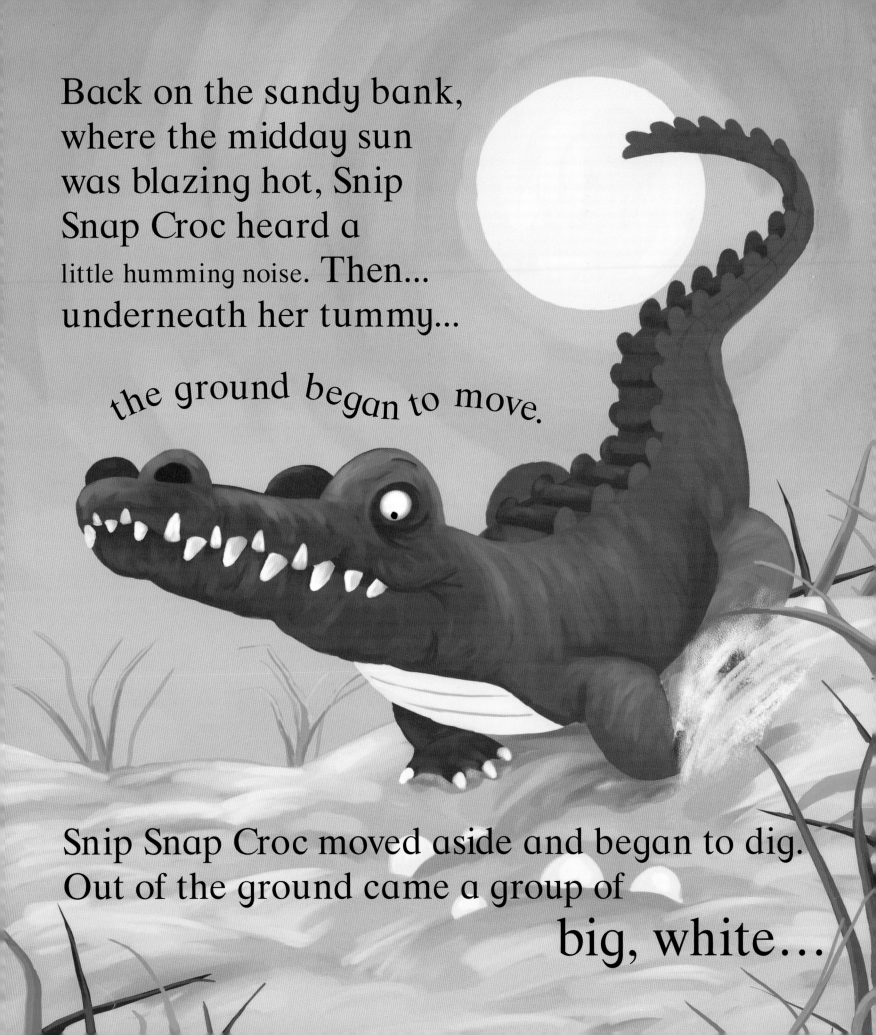

Back on the sandy bank, where the midday sun was blazing hot, Snip Snap Croc heard a little humming noise. Then... underneath her tummy...

the ground began to move.

Snip Snap Croc moved aside and began to dig. Out of the ground came a group of

big, white....

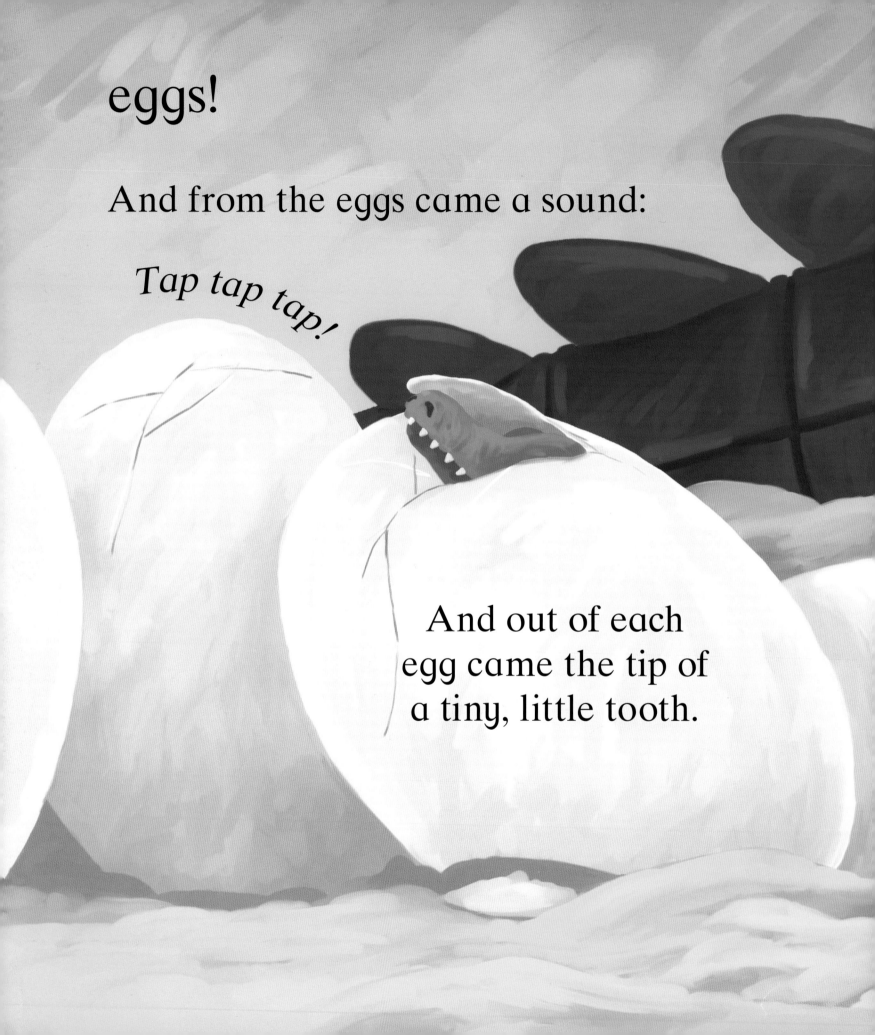

eggs!

And from the eggs came a sound:

Tap tap tap!

And out of each
egg came the tip of
a tiny, little tooth.

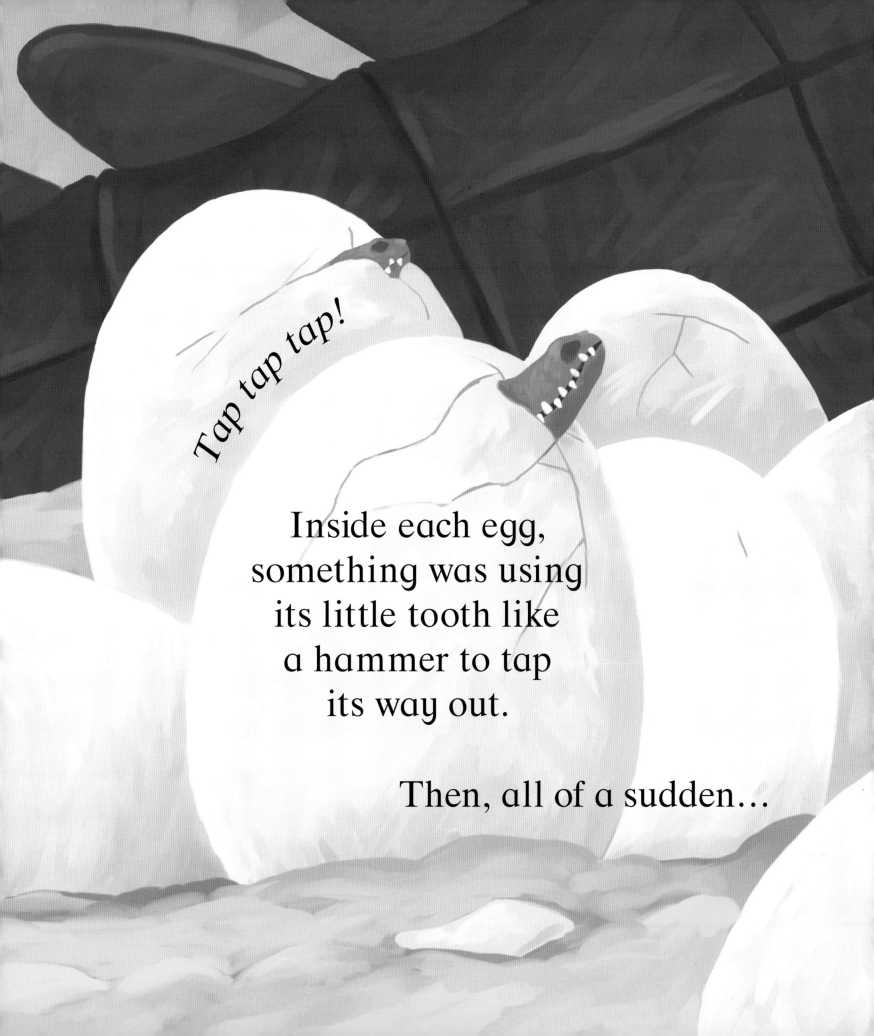

Tap tap tap!

Inside each egg,
something was using
its little tooth like
a hammer to tap
its way out.

Then, all of a sudden…

one,

two,

three,

four,

five,

six,

and more, and more...
baby crocodiles

came wriggling, jiggling onto the shore!

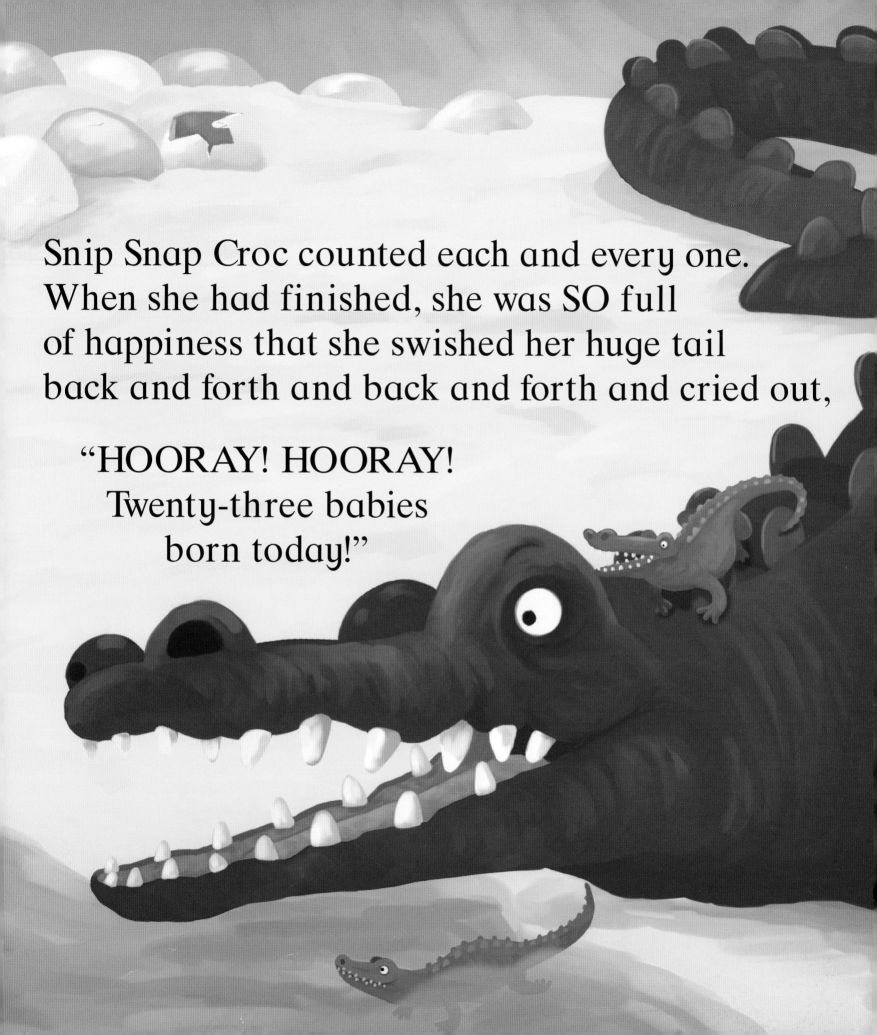

Snip Snap Croc counted each and every one.
When she had finished, she was SO full
of happiness that she swished her huge tail
back and forth and back and forth and cried out,

"HOORAY! HOORAY!
Twenty-three babies
born today!"

Baby Baboon, the baby meerkats, and the two little lion cubs watched from the safety of the riverbank.

They could not believe their eyes. One by one, Snip Snap Croc popped each baby into her mouth!

"Oh, Mama, come quick!" cried Baby Baboon.

"Oh, Mama, over here!" cried the baby meerkats.

"Oh, Mama," cried the lion cubs, "Just *look*!"

"Snip Snap Croc is **eating her babies!**"

But Mama Lion, Mama
Meerkat, and Mama
Baboon knew better.
They knew that Snip
Snap Croc had a secret.

This is what Snip Snap Croc did:
She waddled down to the riverside,
opened her huge mouth, and
very slowly and very carefully
popped each baby into the water!

Then, Snip Snap Croc called out,
"All riverbank creatures, listen to me:
Stay away from my babies twenty-three.
Or by the sky above and the earth beneath,
I will snap you up with my big, sharp teeth."

Mama Snip Snap Croc told her babies,
"Don't stray far from your Mama Croc,
for there are creatures who would eat *you* up.
Stay close by me and no harm you'll meet.
For I love you more than the river deep."

Mama Baboon, Mama Meerkat, and Mama Lion all sighed happily. They knew that although Snip Snap Croc was fierce and dangerous, she wanted to keep her babies safe, just as they did their own.

And they knew she loved each and every one, just as much as they did their own.

Mountain high,
star bright,
ocean wide,
and river deep.

Notes for Teachers and Parents

- Look at the front cover of the book together. Talk about the picture. Can the children guess what the book is going to be about? Read the title together.
- When the children first read the story (or had it read to them), how did they think it was going to end? Were they right? How else could the story have ended?
- Ask the children to take turns to try to read the story aloud. Help them with any difficult words and remember to praise the children for their efforts in reading the book.
- Spell out the names of the animals in the book. Ask the children to repeat the spellings each time you read the story together.
- The children can then try and think of words that rhyme with the animals' names. Make lists of these rhyming words.
- Encourage the children to write a short poem about one of the animals. Use your rhyming word lists to help.
- With the children, make up a tune and sing a verse of one of the mother animals' rhymes.
- Play a game, thinking how big, deep, high, etc, love could be. What do all the animals' moms have in common? Discuss how all moms, even the most fierce, love and protect their babies. Encourage the children to talk about what kinds of things their moms (or other caregivers) do to protect them.
- Study a map of the Nile River with the children and choose where Snip Snap Croc might live. This is a good opportunity to talk about Africa. Explain that Africa is a continent and how continents are usually divided into different countries. Can the children name any other continents? Do they know which continent they live in?
- Make a collage of the river and its surroundings. Ask the children to make drawings or paintings of Snip Snap Croc and the other animals in the story. These can then be glued onto the collage. Discuss what other animals may live in the area. For example; giraffe, pelican, hippopotamus, or eagle.